D1536802

Barty's Ketchup Catastrophe

For Paul

First published in Great Britain in 1999
by Piccadilly Press Ltd.,
5 Castle Road, London NW1 8PR

Designed by Louise Millar
Printed and bound in Belgium by Proost
Set in Sabon 30pt

ISBN: 1 85340 484 5 (paperback)
EAN: 9 781853 404849

3 5 7 9 10 8 6 4 2

A catalogue record of this book is available from the British Library

Sally Chambers lives in Hayes, Kent.
She has written and illustrated a number of picture books,
including these books for Piccadilly Press:

TOFFEE IN TROUBLE

TOFFEE TAKES A NAP

TOFFEE'S NEW FRIEND

TOFFEE'S NIGHT NOISES

WILBIE – FOOTIE MAD!

WILBIE FINDS A FRIEND

WILBIE AND HARRY

Find out more at www.piccadillypress.co.uk

Barty's Ketchup Catastrophe

Sally Chambers

Piccadilly Press • London

Barty loved ketchup.
He had it with everything.

He had it for breakfast.

He had it for lunch.

He had it for dinner.

He even had it . . .
for his birthday!

Barty's family thought he was crazy –
"Crazy for ketchup!" they all said.

Barty always had to
help his mum with
the shopping as the
ketchup was heavy.

His friend Cedric hated ketchup. At lunch-time he always brought a peanut butter sandwich for Barty. Barty always put ketchup on it.

One day Cedric invited Barty to a
sleep-over at his house. For the first time
ever Barty's parents said that he could go.

Barty was really excited.

That day Barty packed and repacked all the things

he would need for his sleep-over at Cedric's.

When he got there he raced up to
Cedric's room and they played

games,

cards

and
puzzles.   Then it was time for dinner . . .

Cedric's family was having one of Barty's favourites – grass pizza!

"Can I have the ketchup, please?"
asked Barty.
"Oh. I don't think we have any,"
said Cedric's mum.

NO KETCHUP!

What a catastrophe!
What was Barty to do?

First of all he watched
everyone else eat.

Then he drank all his drink.

Then he thought he would cry, but he was in Cedric's house.

Finally he thought he would try one little piece.

Then he tried another one and another one.
And then he asked for seconds.
It was quite good really, even if it needed ketchup.

And at breakfast the next morning,
Barty didn't even worry about
not having ketchup for his cereal!

When he got home, everyone thought Barty was cured of his ketchup craze!

But the next time he slept over at Cedric's there was one thing he didn't forget to pack . . .